THE LOSERS
FIGHT BACK

Barbara M. Joosse

THE LOSERS
FIGHT BACK

A WILD WILLIE MYSTERY

Illustrated by Sue Truesdell

A Yearling Book

Published by
Bantam Doubleday Dell Books for Young Readers
a division of
Bantam Doubleday Dell Publishing Group, Inc.
1540 Broadway
New York, New York 10036

ISBN: 0-440-41110-6

Reprinted by arrangement with Houghton Mifflin Company

Printed in the United States of America

June 1996

10 9 8 7 6 5 4 3 2 1

CWO

Contents

• 1 •

Kicking Butt

Lucy and I got to the field a half hour before the game. Coach blew his whistle. "Okay, team. We're going to run a drill. Take turns kicking on goal. Remember to concentrate. Remember to *power kick*." Then he threw a ball toward the first kid in line, Mikey.

Mikey kicked. He missed the goal.

"Kick harder," Coach yelled.

Lucy kicked. Her shot dribbled in.

"Kick harder," Coach yelled.

Derek was next. But Derek was picking dandelions and rubbing the yellow stuff on his chin.

"Derek! DEREK! Pay attention! Kick the ball," Coach yelled.

Derek kicked, but the ball missed the goal by a mile.

"Come on in, team," Coach yelled. We jammed around Coach. "Listen, guys," he said. "We're not doing very well this season."

"We stink," said Mikey.

"Now, Mikey, I wouldn't say that, exactly." Coach rubbed at his whiskers.

2

"We're getting better," Lucy said.

"Yes," Coach said. "So today I want you to give that extra effort. I want you to concentrate. I want you to power kick at the goal."

"This time," I said, "we'll kick butt."

"YES!" Lucy yelled. She punched her arm in the air. She started chanting. "Kick butt! Kick butt! Kick butt!"

Everybody started yelling.

"We're great!" I yelled.

"We're mean," Derek yelled.

"We're the Bruisers!" Lucy yelled.

I centered up for the kickoff and I creamed the ball. But something went wrong and the ball got stuck at the Tornados' halfback. A big guy, real big. The halfback kicked the ball, and it sailed right

over my head. Their forward started dribbling and headed right for the goal.

But he wouldn't make it. No way. Our goalie would stop it. We were going to kick butt.

Something went wrong. The ball got in.

Then the big halfback moved up to forward. Whenever that big guy got the ball, he kept it. Nobody could get it away from him. The big guy made two goals. I was glad when the whistle blew for half-time.

Lucy and I headed for the oranges. Lucy stuck one between her lips and smiled a juicy orange-smile.

I sucked on my section. "In the *first* half," I said, "we were just warming up. We're going to be great in the *second* half."

Then somebody started yelling, "Losers! Losers!" It was Chuckie Herman. He had this ugly look on his face. And he was laughing at us.

Chuckie is big, real big. He has little, squinty eyes and hair that's cut so short you can see the skin through it. His legs are like tree trunks. He wears clunky motorcycle boots. Everybody's afraid of Chuckie, including me.

Lucy clenched her hand into a fist. "That slimeface," she said. "He's laughing at us! I'm going to tell him to lay off."

"Are you kidding?" I said. "Let me give you some advice, free of charge. Never, ever cross Chuckie Herman."

"Says who?" said Lucy. She stomped up to Chuckie and made the biggest mistake of her life. "Get a life, Chuck Herman," she yelled. I couldn't believe she said that! Lucy was dead meat.

Chuckie stared at Lucy with a stupid look on his face. I don't know of a single person who has ever talked back to Chuckie, until Lucy. What would he do to her?

"Do you even *play* soccer?" she yelled. Lucy's face was red and she was leaning forward. Her hands were in fists.

"I'm not on a team," said Chuckie, sneering.

"You're *afraid* to play, aren't you? You're afraid you aren't any good. That's it, isn't it?"

Chuckie snorted. "Me? Not very good? You've gotta be kidding. I'm the best soccer player you ever saw. I just choose not to play on a team."

"Why not?" Lucy asked. "You're nothing but a chicken!" I began to picture Lucy at her funeral. She was too young to die. I ran over to Lucy to save her.

But Chuckie laughed. "Well, you're nothing but a girl."

Lucy was my friend. I had to say something. "She's . . . she's . . ." But I couldn't think of anything to say. Chuckie was right. Lucy *was* a girl.

I stood up to Chuckie. I said, "Lucy's not a regular girl. She's different."

"Woo-oo-oooo," Chuckie said, wiggling his eyebrows and swerving his hips.

Coach came up. "Settle down, guys, or we'll get red-flagged."

We went back to eating oranges. When I bit mine, I pretended it was Chuckie Herman.

The second half started. The second
half ended. The score was six–zip. The
Tornados were the six and we were the
zip.

I kicked the ball because I was angry. It dribbled over to Chuckie. Chuckie booted it, hard. The ball really took off. It flew through the air, halfway across the soccer field.

"Haw haw haw!" laughed Chuckie. "You're nothing but a bunch of losers. Hey, I know," he said, snapping his fingers. "You can change your name. You can change it from the Bruisers to the Losers."

Names like that have a way of sticking.

• 2 •

Secret Plan

I woke up with the sound of small bullets in my ear. *Ping. Ping.* I dove under the covers.

Ping. Ping. I stuck my head out. It wasn't small bullets. It was stones on my window. I stepped over my Space Mutant guys and went to the window. It was Lucy.

"Can I come in?" she said.

I crouched down below the windowsill. "I'm in my pajamas, and you're a girl," I explained.

"So what?" said Lucy. "I've seen my dad

in pajamas lots of times. It doesn't matter to me."

I thought about it. "It matters to me. Wait there while I change."

Which I did. "Now you can come in."

Lucy came in through my open window. She shoved the space guys aside and sat on the floor cross-legged. "Come here," she said, leaning toward me. "This is secret."

"Okay. I'm listening."

"We're on a losing team. After Chuckie Herman started it, everybody's calling us the Losers. I don't like to be on a losing team."

"Who does?"

"So I want to *do* something about it. I just haven't figured out what."

I walked around in a circle, like television detectives do when they have a big problem.

"Have you thought of anything yet?" she asked me after a while.

"No, have you?" I asked.

"No." I kept walking.

Suddenly, we looked at each other and said, "Let's call the King."

King Kyle is my old best friend. When he moved to stupid-Cleveland-stupid-Ohio we formed a detective agency: Wild Willie, Lucky Lucy, and King Kyle, Detectives. Sometimes Kyle helps us solve problems.

Lucy and I crammed into the hall closet

together so we could talk without anyone hearing. It was hot in the closet, but it was private.

I punched the King's number. "Yo! Kyle Krane here," he said into the phone.

"KYLE!" I yelled.

"WILLIE!" he yelled. "So how's good old Grafton?"

"Still here," I said. "How's Cleveland?"

"Still stupid," he said.

Lucy grabbed the phone away from me. "Kyle, we've got a problem."

"Ah," said Kyle, "detective business."

"Right. We're on this soccer team, the

Bruisers. Only we really stink, so everyone's calling us the Losers."

I grabbed the phone away from Lucy. "We want to be a hot team. But how?"

"Hmm," said Kyle. "Hmmmm." I waited for him to have a brainstorm. "I'VE GOT IT!" he yelled. "Am I brilliant, or what? All you have to do is figure out why the other guys win!"

"RIGHT!" I yelled. Then I said goodbye. "Up your nose with a rubber hose."

Kyle said good-bye. "In your pants with fire ants."

What a guy.

"So what did he say?" asked Lucy, pushing the closet door open.

"He said we have to figure out why the other teams win."

Lucy's eyes got skinny. "That's it? *That's* his big idea? It doesn't sound like much to me."

I held out my hands. "Just listen," I said. "We need to watch the other teams. We need to figure out what makes them win and us lose."

"I get it! Winning teams have something in common, right? Like they all chew Juicy Fruit gum before a game," cried Lucy.

"Or they do twenty-one jumping jacks."

"Or they wear purple shin guards."

"YES!" I said, running my hand through my sweaty hair. "But if they catch us watching, they'll kick us out."

Lucy jabbed a finger into my chest. "They won't kick us out because they

won't know it's *us*. We'll wear disguises."

I scruffled my hair with my hand. "This is going to be great!"

"Willie!" Lucy said. "Your hair is sticking out all over. You look like Ronald McDonald."

I climbed over some toys to look in my mirror. "You're right."

"It looks wild," said Lucy.

I grinned and got a pen and paper. "The first thing we have to do is get a practice schedule for a bunch of teams. You get two schedules and I'll get two. Then we'll meet here at exactly four o'clock."

"Roger," said Lucy, using detective talk. Then she left the way she came, through the window.

Now we were getting somewhere. I felt great. I took a shower and washed my hair. Then I wrapped a towel around myself and stood in front of the bathroom mirror. I put a lot of gel in my hair and puffed it out with my hand. Now I really looked like Wild Willie.

· 3 ·

K-i-s-s-i-n-g

Lucy and I met on her front porch. "Did you get the schedules?" I asked her.

"Yup. I got one for the Kickers and one for the Stars."

I waved my papers in the air. "I got one for the Blasters and one for the Tigers. The Tigers are really hot. Is anybody practicing this afternoon?"

"The Kickers are practicing in a half hour. If we hurry, we can make it."

Suddenly, this loud voice yelled, "Hey, Willie!"

I looked up. There was Chuckie.

Chuckie made this loud, wet kissing noise. *Sllurp.* Then he sang:

Willie and Lucy sitting in a tree
K-I-S-S-I-N-G
first comes love
then comes marriage
then comes Lucy in a baby carriage
suckin' her thumb
wettin' her pants
doin' the hula hula dance.

Lucy ran up to Chuckie before I could stop her. Her lips were squeezed together. Little bolts of lightning came out of her eyes. "You're a scumface, Chuck Herman," she said.

Chuckie laughed. "Better go back to your boyfriend, little girl," he said, and rode off on his bike.

Oooooh! Lucy wasn't my girlfriend. But Chuckie thought she was and he'd tell

everybody. Then everyone would think
we were kissing each other and getting
married. Lucy was my friend, but now I
didn't want anyone to see us together.

"Hey, Lucy," I said. "I feel kind of hot out here. Do you want to go inside?"

Lucy put her hands on her hips. "You want to go inside because of that K-I-S-S-I-N-G song, don't you?"

I gulped. "Yes."

"Chuckie Herman is nothing but a scumface," Lucy said. "Who cares what he thinks?"

"I do," I said. "Because if he thinks you're my girlfriend, then he'll tell other people. Pretty soon everybody will think we're kissing."

"No offense, Willie," Lucy said, "but I'd rather kiss a lizard. You're my friend, not my *boyfriend*."

"I know that and you know that, but what will everybody else think?"

Lucy looked at me. "All right. I think it's stupid, but if you want to go inside, let's go."

Inside, Lucy started pulling wigs and

costumes out of her disguise box. "I'm
going to be Francine, the French girl."
Lucy used a French accent. "Now I put on
ze sunglasses and ze hat. Now I walk Fren-
chy, like zis." Lucy put her hands on her
hips and tilted her head back. She looked
at me. "What are you going to be?"

What if Chuckie recognized us even
when we wore the disguises? "Um . . . I
think I'll just go home. You'd better check
out the teams by yourself."

Lucy said, "Aren't you ever going to go outside with me?"

I shrugged. "I guess not. We'll just be inside friends."

"What about our detective agency? What about spying together?"

"We'll still be a detective agency," I explained. "We'll just work together inside. We'll have to spy alone."

Lucy said, "That sounds stupid."

It was, but I didn't know what else to do.

"Well, I'd better go," Lucy said.

I watched her walk down the sidewalk, sneaking behind bushes whenever she could. Sometimes she'd spin around to see if anyone was trailing her.

I walked past Dad, who was washing his car in the driveway. "Hi, sport," he said. "What are you up to?"

"I don't know," I said.

"Do you want to help me wash the car?"

Usually, I liked washing the car. I liked squirting the car and myself and sometimes Dad. I don't know why, but I didn't feel like it today. "No, I'm going inside," I said.

"Okay," Dad said, spraying the car with water.

While Lucy wore this great disguise, I poked holes in my too-small pajamas with a pencil. While Lucy spied on a hot team, I changed the newspapers in the bird cage. While Lucy figured out some kind of master plan, I played tic-tac-toe with myself. When you play tic-tac-toe with yourself, you always win. But you always lose, too.

· 4 ·

No Fun

I watched for Lucy through the window. When she came back from spying, she didn't come right over to my house. I waited, but she still didn't come. I called her on the phone.

"What did you find out?" I asked her.

"I don't think I should tell you on the phone," she said.

"Why not?" I asked.

"Maybe the phone is tapped. I'll be over after I ride my bike." Then she hung up.

I watched through the window as Lucy

dragged some bricks out of the garage and tilted some boards on them. I watched while she got on her bike and flew off the boards. "Yee-ha!" she yelled. It really looked like fun.

After a while, she brought out lemonade. I love lemonade. She sipped it through a bendable straw. Then she took an Oreo and twisted the top off. She licked the white part with her tongue and then ate the cookie part. I love Oreos.

Then Mikey came over. Lucy and Mikey made a goal out of garbage cans. Then they started dribbling the ball.

Every time Lucy made a goal, she shouted.

Every time Mikey made a goal, he shouted.

It was getting too noisy out there so I turned on the TV. I watched it all afternoon. After a while, all the shows started to look the same. In the beginning, I could tell which was which. But then they started to turn into this one, big, boring show.

I hung from the back of the couch with my legs and started watching TV upside down. I started kicking the wall with my stocking feet during commercials. I started counting how many kicks were in each commercial. Some commercials took 120 kicks. I never knew there were so many kicks in a commercial.

"Willie!" Mom said from the kitchen. "What are you doing?"

"Kicking the wall," I said.

"I knew that." Mom poked her head into the living room. "I just wondered if there was a particular reason you were kicking the wall."

"Yes," I said, wriggling up straight. "It's because TV is boring."

Mom came up to me and felt my forehead. "Oh, my!" she said. Then she went "tsk-tsk-tsk" with her tongue. "I'm afraid you have it."

"What?" I asked.

"Well, your face is very pale. In fact, I'm not sure you have any blood at all. That's one of the symptoms." Mom looked at me with a worried expression on her face. "What you have is a bad case of cartoonhead."

"Cartoonhead?" I asked. "You're making that up."

"No, it's a real thing," Mom said. "It's when a boy has watched too much TV and can't think of anything more fun than to kick the wall."

"Oh," I said.

Mom gave me a stern look. "Which, by the way, isn't okay to do, no matter how much cartoonhead you have." She sat down next to me. "Where's Lucy?" she asked.

"Outside. Doing stunts on her bike and drinking lemonade and playing soccer with Mikey."

"Sounds like fun," Mom said. "Why

aren't you playing with her?"

"Because Chuckie thinks she's my girl-friend. And if he sees us together he'll tease us."

"I see," Mom said. I wondered if she really did. "If he saw you having fun to-gether, it's hard to say what he'd do. He might . . . talk about it. Now that would be really awful. No, it's much better to stay inside and watch TV. I can see that."

While I watched the gajillionth show, I wrote a letter to Kyle:

Dear King,

My life is full of problems:

1) The team problem
2) Chuckie thinks Lucy is my girlfriend (which she is NOT!)
3) He'll tell the whole, entire world
4) Now I have to stay inside so no one can see us together
5) There are too many dumb shows on TV.

I can only think of one solution. I'm moving to stupid—Cleveland—stupid—Ohio. Move over.

Detectively yours,

Wild Willie

Private Investigator

38

• 5 •

Spying on the Tigers

After one more show, Lucy came. She had on huge sunglasses and a floppy hat. She was carrying a notebook.

"What did you find out?" I asked.

Lucy took off her sunglasses, then her hat, then she found a comfortable spot to sit, then she leaned back in her seat.

"Lucy!" I groaned. "Can't you go any faster?"

Slowly, slowly, Lucy turned each page in her notebook until she got to the right

one. She cleared her throat. "First, I watched the Kickers. The Kickers aren't that hot. But they have one kid who's really good, and he scores all the points."

"What about the Blasters?" I asked.

"They aren't that hot, either. Most of the kids on the team are just okay. But they have one big guy. This kid is big, real big, and he can kick the ball halfway across the field. He can kick it over the heads of the other kids and score a goal."

"Like the Tornados," I said, running my hand through my wild hair. "Maybe what the winning teams have in common is one big guy."

Lucy smiled. "Maybe. But I think I should spy on another team. We need to know for sure."

"Are you going to wear a disguise again?" I asked.

"Yup. I'm going to wear a skateboarder's disguise."

Boy, it really sounded like fun.

"If Chuckie saw us in our disguises," I said slowly, "he wouldn't know it was us, would he?"

"Right," Lucy said.

"I'm going," I said, jumping up.

Lucy and I wore neon clothes and went to the practice field on skateboards.

At the field, we watched the best team in the league, the Tigers. You could tell right away who their best player was. Number 3. His big head stuck up above all the other players. He wasn't fast, but he was strong. When he got the ball, he really creamed it. The ball blasted into the air like it was shot from a gun. BANG! It went halfway across the field. Sometimes

he missed the goal, and sometimes he got it in. But nobody could stop him.

Lucy and I looked at each other.

"That's it," she said.

"The thing that makes a winning team is . . ." I said.

"One Big Guy," we both said together.

"How come all the other teams have a big guy, and we don't?" Lucy asked.

I thought about that for a while. I paced, to help me think better. "At the beginning of the season, the coaches pick guys for a team. But our coach is new. He probably didn't know you have to get a big guy to win."

Lucy nodded. Then she asked the biggest question of all, the one I'd been wondering about myself. "Where are we going to get One Big Guy?"

One Big Guy

We definitely needed to call Kyle. We were a team, and when a team solved a big problem, they did it together. Lucy and I crammed in our closet–phone booth and punched his number.

The King answered. "Yo! Krane residence, also the Cleveland branch of the King Kyle Detective Agency."

"Kyle," I said, "it's the Wild Willie, Lucky Lucy, and King Kyle Detective Agency—not what you said."

"Right," Kyle said. "I just thought I'd shorten it. Anyway, have you figured out what makes the other teams win?"

"Yes," I said. "It's . . ."

Lucy grabbed the phone away from me. "It's One Big Guy. Every single winning team has one guy who's big . . ."

I grabbed the phone from Lucy. "And he scores all the points. Everybody else just stands there, trying to stay out of the way."

Lucy grabbed it back. "Sometimes the Big Guy misses, but if he aims right, no-

body can stop the ball. It flies over everybody's head and gets in."

I took the phone again and covered the receiver with my hand. "Lucy," I said, "this is my phone, so I get to finish talking."

"Okay," she said. "As long as we call from my house the next time, and *I* can talk."

I began. "So, King, everybody on our team is regular-sized. We really need One Big Guy. But who?"

"You're not going to like this," said Kyle.

I had a terrible, terrible feeling.

"Chuckie," Kyle said.

My heart felt like chewed-up meat with fat in it, and it fell into my knees and I got very hot. "I was afraid you'd say that," I said. Then I said to Lucy, "He said to get Chuckie."

Lucy groaned.

"Well, you want to win, don't you?" asked Kyle.

"Yes," I said.

"Then Chuckie's the guy. Nobody's bigger or tougher."

Suddenly, I didn't feel like talking anymore. I felt like packing my suitcase and moving to Cleveland. "I'd better go," I said.

"In your ear with a horse's rear," he said.

I just said good-bye. Gross things aren't so funny when your stomach feels like glop. I hung up.

"Kyle's right," said Lucy. "We've got to get Chuckie. But how are we going to talk him into it?"

"Yeah," I said. "I was thinking of that, too. He might cream us just for asking."

"Well, we've got to try. Let's go."

"Yeah," I said. "Let's." We both stayed in the closet.

"Maybe we should have some ice cream first."

Lucy and I scooped out mint ice cream and poured lots of chocolate on top. Then we mixed it up.

"Red-hots would be good in it," Lucy said, adding some.

"And some little marshmallows."

We mixed them all together and had this great snack. We called it chocolate soup, and here is the recipe:

—LOTS OF ICE CREAM, ANY FLAVOR

—LOTS OF CHOCOLATE SYRUP

—SOME RED-HOTS, BUT PUT THEM IN THE CHOCO-LATE SOUP BEFORE THEY MELT IN YOUR HAND

—SOME MARSHMALLOWS

MIX WITH YOUR SPOON UNTIL IT LOOKS LIKE CHUNKY SOUP. THEN EAT.

We couldn't put it off any longer. We had to go to Chuckie's.

• 7 •

Big Bucks

As we walked to Chuckie's, I really wanted to hold Lucy's hand. I was scared to talk to Chuckie, and it would feel good. But I was worried someone would see us.

Lucy rang the doorbell. We waited for somebody to answer. When no one did, we began to walk away. Just then, Chuckie stuck his head out of the upstairs window and said, "What d'ya want?"

"We wanted to talk to you," Lucy said. "Could you come down?"

"Yuh." Chuckie threw a rope out of the window and began to climb down. His big feet landed with a solid thud. Feet like that could kick a ball to Canada.

"So what did you want, anyway?" asked Chuckie.

Lucy and I looked at each other. She was hoping I'd talk, and I was hoping she would. She started. "Well, Chuck, you know we're on this team, the Bruisers."

Chuckie snorted. "The Losers, you mean."

"Well," I said, "we haven't won a lot of games . . ."

"You haven't won *any* games," Chuckie reminded me.

"All right, then, we haven't won any games. But we could. We're just missing something."

Lucy said, "One Big Guy. See, Willie and I spied on some teams. We spied until we figured out what makes the other teams win and our team lose. And the winning thing is One Big Guy. Coach said it was okay to add a new player . . ."

Chuckie cackled. "This is great! So

you're looking for One Big Guy to join your team and you were hoping it would be me?"

This was going to be easier than I thought. "Yes," I said.

"Well," he said. "I think something can be arranged."

"Hey," I said. "That's great. You'll join the team?"

"Maybe," Chuckie said. "You know

how the Brewers get the top players, don't you?"

"A little," Lucy said.

"And you know these top players don't play for nothing, right?"

"What do you mean?" I asked.

"What I mean, Willie, is that a really *valuable* player gets big bucks."

Lucy and I looked at each other. My eyebrows shot up into my forehead. "Big bucks? We don't even have little bucks. We can't pay you, Chuckie."

Chuckie sat on a lawn chair and crossed his legs. "Of course you don't have tons of money, but you get an allowance, don't you?"

I covered my pocket with my hand. "Sure, but not a lot."

"Me neither," said Lucy.

"How much do you get?" Chuckie asked.

Now here was a problem. I know that lying is a bad thing. But I also knew that if I told Chuckie I got three dollars a week, he'd want the whole thing. So I lied. But I crossed my fingers. "Two dollars."

"Me, too," said Lucy. I knew Lucy got four.

Chuckie snorted. "Boy, your parents are cheapskates!" Chuckie's eyes got skinny. "You aren't lying to the Chuckster, are you?" he asked.

Lucy shook her head no, and so did I.

"Well, then, that's how much it's going

to take to get me on the team. Four bucks
a week." Chuckie smiled.

Lucy whispered into my ear, "I really
want to win. I think we should do it."

"Deal," I said, sticking out my hand to
shake Chuckie's.

Chuckie shook my hand and then Lucy's. "You won't be sorry," he said.

But it was too late. I already was.

Dear Willie,

Yow! You sure have some problems. Here's my advice:

1) The team problem. We already figured this out.

2—4) Problem with Chuckie thinking Lucy is your girlfriend. I specialize in sports and mysteries.

5) Dumb TV shows. Put yellow plastic over the screen. It will make everyone look sick. It's hysterical.

I think you should move to Cleveland, too. Then it wouldn't be stupid anymore.

Detectively yours,

King Kyle

Private Investigator

◆ 8 ◆

Chuckie's Game

Right away, I could tell who was going to win. Our teams had lined up for the kickoff. Both of us had One Big Guy. Ours was bigger than theirs.

Chuckie played center forward. The ref placed the ball on the center line and Chuckie stepped up to it. He looked at the ball. Then he looked at the other players, one by one. I heard this funny sound coming from Chuckie, like a dog growling. The other team backed up and Chuckie kicked.

I have never seen a ball fly before, but this one did. It smashed away from

Chuckie's foot like it was running for its life. It flew through the air and landed close to the goal.

Lucy and I ran up to the ball and started to fight the other team for it. All of a sudden this absolutely huge leg reached over the others and kicked the ball. It was

Chuckie. WHANG! Chuckie kicked the ball right into the goal. The goalie didn't stand a chance.

We got the point, so the other team got to kick off. Their Big Guy was the kicker. He stood in front of Chuckie. He narrowed his eyes into thin little slits.

Chuckie walked up closer. Now their toes were touching. Chuckie looked at the kid . . . and Chuckie laughed.

The kid's face got very red. He turned around and backed off for the kickoff. He ran up to the ball and kicked. But he kicked too hard, and he tripped and fell on his butt. All the kids started laughing, but Chuckie just smiled.

After that, it was Chuckie's game. Chuckie didn't run very much. I guess he didn't like to sweat. But the truth is, he

didn't have to. If he ever got to the ball at all, nobody got it away from him. He was the biggest, toughest guy of all. And we were the Bruisers!

At half, the score was three–one. For the first time, we were winning.

I headed for the oranges. Lucy was already there, making faces with an orange section in her mouth. She was laugh-

ing like crazy. I really wanted to punch
Lucy on the shoulder. I really wanted
to say, "Hey, Luce, great game, huh?"
But if I did, Chuckie might see us and sing
the K-I-S-S-I-N-G song. So I just watched
her laughing and being silly without me.

I walked up to Derek and said, "Hey,
Derek, isn't this the best?"

Derek was kicking some dirt into a pile
and then jumping on it. He looked at me
and said, "Huh?"

"This game," I said. "It's great to be winning!"

Derek said, "Sure. Wanna help me stomp on the dirt?" Derek was a little spacey. Maybe he didn't understand about winning.

So I ate another orange section by myself and watched Lucy.

"C'mon, team," Coach said, and we huddled around. "Great first half," he said, grinning.

"YES!" Lucy yelled.

"Keep this up and I'll buy sodas for everyone."

"ALL RIGHT!" I yelled.

He gave us each our new positions. He kept Chuckie as forward.

It was the best game of my life. The Bruisers scored a total of five points. The other team scored two. At last, we had kicked butt.

After the game, Coach bought us sodas.

Lucy was sitting at another table, and I thought how great it would be to tell her a joke with soda in her mouth. It would be great to make her laugh so hard that the soda would fizz up her nose.

But she was a girl, and I didn't want anybody to see us having fun together.

Chuckie leaned over my chair. He yawned. He said, "Willie, I'm awful tired. See, I've got all this work to do at home. Mow the lawn. Collect the empty bottles."

"Yeah?" I said.

"And that really worries me," Chuckie said, leaning an elbow on my shoulder. "See, I really should save my energy for the game on Thursday. But if I do all this work, see, I'm afraid I'll be too tired to play."

I gulped hard, and the soda fizzed in my stomach.

"So I was thinking. Maybe you could

mow the lawn and Lucy could collect all the empty bottles."

"What would you be doing?"

"I'd be resting." Chuckie smiled. "For the game."

Kyle,

Things are worse. Now Lucy and I have to do Chuckie's work for him.

I figured out the girl thing myself. I made up some rules:

1) You can be *seen* with a girl
2) But never bump her on the arm
3) Never kiss a girl, not even your mom
4) Moms can kiss *you,* if they have dry lips
5) Only be friends with sporty-girls, not girly-girls
6) Get married when you are old.

You can use my rules if you want.

Solvingly yours,

Wild Willie

Private Investigator

◆ 9 ◆

Payola

"**W**here are you going?" Mom asked.

"To mow the lawn," I answered.

Mom looked confused. "That's funny," she said. "You just mowed our lawn yesterday."

"I know," I said. "I'm not mowing our lawn, I'm mowing Chuckie's."

Mom sat on the couch. "Well, that's very nice of you. It's good to see you developing such a nice friendship."

"It isn't exactly friendship," I said. "It's more like ownership."

"What do you mean?" Mom asked.

I blew air through my lips and made them sputter like a wet balloon. "BE-CAUSE," I said, "I have to pay Chuckie to play on our team."

"Oh?" Mom said.

"See, part of the pay is doing his work for him. I'm mowing and Lucy is collecting his empty bottles. Another part of the pay is money—four bucks a week."

"Hmm," Mom said. "Willie, have you ever heard of payola?"

"Is that one of those kid games advertised on TV?"

Mom looked at me seriously. "No, Willie. It's blackmail. It's when you want something so badly you pay someone to make it happen even though you know it is wrong."

I sat next to Mom on the couch. Mom kissed my hair, where I was used to it. "Willie, the thing about payola is that the price keeps going up. You have to keep paying more and more."

I sighed. It felt nice, sitting next to Mom. Mom bent down to kiss me but then she remembered I don't like kisses on my face and she stopped. "I'm sorry," she said. "I almost forgot."

I looked at Mom. "I don't mean to be rotten about kisses," I said. "If you kissed me real quick, it might be okay. Like this." I touched my finger to my hand, quickly, to show her how fast her kiss would have to be. "And no lipstick, and dry lips."

"Let me try," Mom said. She dried her lips with her hand and bent down. Then she kissed me very, very quickly. It wasn't too bad.

I jumped off the couch. "Gotta go," I said.

I put a note in Lucy's mailbox about more payola and headed for Chuckie's.

Chuckie was on his front porch. He was on a rocker. He was drinking something. "The mower's in the garage," he yelled.

I began to mow. The sun was hot. Very hot. "What are you drinking?" I asked.

"Lemonade. With ice. It's very good." Chuckie made a loud slurping noise with his straw.

I mowed. There weren't any clouds in the sky, and I started wishing for clouds. I started wishing for rain. If it would rain, I could quit mowing. I wiped my sweaty forehead with my arm.

"Don't slow down," Chuckie yelled from the porch.

I figured I'd be mowing Chuckie's lawn for the rest of my life. Payola, I thought, stinks.

· 10 ·

The Chucksters

Another game. Chuckie played center forward. Lucy and I played right and left wings. We were winning. Again.

Why didn't I feel good about it?

Some poor halfback had just kicked the ball within the Chuck-zone. Chuckie grabbed it with his foot. He dribbled downfield. Everybody kind of let him have the ball and let him get the goal. It was the third goal of the game. He had made the other two.

At half, Coach said, "Chuck, you really are a great forward, but soccer is a team sport. You've got to pass the ball."

"You mean kick the ball to someone else?" Chuckie looked offended.

"Yes. I'm going to put you in as right wing. Watch for a chance to pass, and then kick the ball to one of your teammates."

"Sure, Coach," Chuckie said.

The second half started, and Chuckie got the ball right away. He dribbled downfield. I ran next to him, waiting for him to pass.

But Chuckie didn't pass.

I was wide open. I was in front of the goal, and nobody was in my way. If Chuckie passed to me I *know* I could have made a goal. I would have creamed it. BAM! But Chuckie didn't pass.

Way from the side, Chuckie kicked toward the goal. It was stupid, because he was too far away and the goal was at a terrible angle. The ball bounced off the goalpost. It was out.

I looked at Lucy. Her eyes were skinny and her mouth was squeezed together. She knew what I knew: *I could have made that goal, and Chuckie didn't let me.* It was like Chuckie was the whole team. He never let anybody else get the ball—not if he could help it. Winning isn't much fun when you never get to play.

After the game, Chuckie smiled his fake smile. "Lucy and Willie, I really want to buy some baseball cards and I don't have enough money. I need another dollar."

Chuckie held out his hand for the money. I put in forty cents and Lucy put in forty-five cents. He kept his hand out, waiting for the rest.

"It's all I have," I explained.

"Me, too," said Lucy.

Chuckie jiggled his hand. "That's too bad, because I need a whole dollar for the baseball cards. See, baseball cards make me happy. And a happy Chuckie is a good soccer player. Get it?"

"We do, but this is all we have."

"I suppose I can wait a day for the rest," Chuckie said. "You can pay me fifteen cents tomorrow."

At bedtime, I combed my hair flat. I didn't feel like Wild Willie anymore. Then I lay in bed, thinking. Saturday was a big game. If we won, we would be champions. I was staring at the ceiling, trying to feel good about winning, when I heard a noise.

Plink. Klink. It was pebbles on my window. I got up from bed and whispered, "Yeah?" as I opened the window.

Lucy was standing there in her pajamas. It was very dark except for the streetlights.

"I'm in my pajamas, and you're a girl," I reminded her.

"I'm coming in anyway," she said. "You can put on a robe or something."

Lucy climbed inside. "We've got to talk about Chuckie."

Lucy and I sat on the bed, which was the only place we could sit, considering all the stuff on the floor. "That reminds me," I said. "You're supposed to take out the garbage for him, first thing in the morning."

Lucy made a little exploding sound. "That's what I mean," she said. "Think about it. Last week I had to clean his hamster cage."

"I had to wash his bike," I said.

"And Willie, we aren't the Bruisers anymore. Everybody's calling us the Chucksters. It's like he *owns* the team or something," Lucy said.

I looked at her. "Well, let's face it, if we want to keep on winning, we have to do what Chuckie says."

"But he keeps asking for more. And I'm getting sick of it."

"Payola," I said. "Mom said with payola, you have to keep paying more and more."

"I wouldn't mind so much," Lucy said, "if winning was fun. But it isn't fun when Chuckie makes all the goals. We might as well not be on the team."

I sighed.

Lucy said, "What are we going to do?"

"Eat something," I said. "Mom bought a box of Star Zonkers."

Star Zonkers was the cereal of Space Mutants. It always made the Mutants stronger and smarter. Maybe it would help us, too.

We walked through the living room. Mom was doing a crossword puzzle. Dad was reading the paper. He looked at Lucy's pajamas. "I didn't know Lucy was staying overnight."

"She's not," I said. "She's only visiting. We have something important to discuss."

"Chuckie's really starting to get to you, isn't he?" Mom said. I nodded.

The creepy thing about Mom is that she can see into my head. It's like I have this window instead of a forehead, and Mom can see what I'm thinking.

"Winning isn't so much fun when you don't win as a team, is it?" Mom said. "Well, I know you two will figure something out."

Dad looked up from his paper. "Teamwork. That's the ticket."

"Yes," Lucy said. Her mouth was in a straight little line.

Mom said, "Why don't you have some of that new cereal I bought? Zonker-something. I bet it'll help you think."

Like I said. Mom can read my mind.

I don't know if it was the Star Zonkers, but Mom was right. We *did* figure something out.

"You know how Chuckie hogs the ball?" I asked Lucy.

"Yup," Lucy said.

I jabbed my spoon at her. "I think that's the answer."

Then, together, we hatched a plan.

Dear King,

Circle tomorrow on your calendar. It's going to be the greatest day of my life. Here's my plan:

1) Eat two bowls of Star Zonkers, for power.
2) Wear sweaty uniform, for luck.
3) Also for luck, do not step on sidewalk cracks, chew two sticks of Juicy Fruit gum, let Mom kiss me on the cheek (with dry lips).
4) Conquer Chuckie.
5) Conquer the Tigers.

Future plans:

1) Be recruited for a professional soccer team.

Your Friend, Partner, and Future
Professional Soccer Player,

Wild Willie

Private Investigator

86

• 11 •

K-i-c-k-i-n-g

Lucy and I walked to the game. Together. I was sick of worrying about Chuckie seeing us together. From now on, I was going to walk with Lucy whenever I felt like it.

"Are you scared the plan won't work?" I asked.

"Yes," Lucy admitted.

"Me, too," I said. I was nervous, and my head was sweaty. I ran my hand through my hair.

"That's better," Lucy said. She looked

my head. "I didn't like it when you had regular hair. I like your wild look."

"It's more me," I admitted.

When we got to the field, most of the team was already there. Chuckie was talking.

"Okay, guys, this'll be a piece of cake. If you get the ball, pass it to me. I'll handle everything. I'll make sure we score."

The team squeezed in their smiles. They were all in on the plan. They knew today was going to be different.

Coach blew his whistle. "Bruisers, this is the biggest game of the year. If we win, we'll be the champions."

The teams lined up. The Bruisers. The Tigers. Our One Big Guy. Their One Big Guy. Chuckie kicked off. BAM! The ball shot from his foot like a rocket, straight into the big legs of their One Big Guy, Number 3.

Number 3 smiled. His smile reminded
me of Chuckie's. Fake. He recovered the
ball and kicked it, hard. BASH! Right into
Chuckie.

Chuckie kicked.

Number 3 kicked.

Chuckie.

Number 3.

The ball kept going back and forth like
a Ping-Pong ball. It wasn't getting any-
where. Then it went foul. The ref blew the
whistle. It was our ball.

Chuckie held the ball in the air, his thick arms swinging it over his head. He narrowed his eyes and stared at old Number 3. Number 3 stared back.

It was like bullets were shooting from their eyes.

It was like there wasn't anybody else in the game. Just Chuckie and Number 3.

By half, the score was zip–zip. The two Big Guys had very red faces. There was sweat all over them. They looked like they'd run a hundred miles and kicked a thousand balls.

I winked at Lucy. "I think old Number 3 is really wiped out."

"Yeah, and Chuckie looks like dead meat, too. They've really paralyzed each other."

Our plan was working perfectly.

After halftime, the team lined up for the kickoff. The Big Guys dragged themselves onto the field. They walked like robots, stiff and slow.

Chuckie kicked. *Boing.* It dinked off the big legs of old Number 3.

This was it! Energy bulged out of my body. I darted in between the big guys and stole the ball. They were too weak to get it back! I dribbled the ball until I ran into a Tiger. Then I passed to Lucy.

She caught it with her foot, neat. *Bing. Bing. Bing.* She dribbled the ball downfield until she ran into a Tiger. She passed to me.

I was in the clear. I was in front of the goal. I trapped the ball. Aimed. Kicked.

A GOAL! A BIG, FAT, INCREDIBLE GOAL!

"YES!" Lucy yelled, shooting her arms in the air.

We clapped hands together. I didn't care if anyone saw us.

The sides lined up again, and the Tigers kicked off. Number 3 kicked, *zooosh*. It was a wimpy kick. He was pooped out.

Lucy got the ball. She dribbled. She passed to me. I wound my way around a few legs, but then a Tiger got it. He was dribbling the ball to their goal when Derek came out of nowhere. *Boing*. He grabbed the ball.

"Mom! Hey, Mom!" he yelled. "I got the ball!" Derek dribbled it some more, and when the Tigers closed in, he passed to Lucy. Lucy was in front of the goal, but Number 3 was between her and the goal.

She shot, and Number 3 went for the ball,
but he was too slow and he missed. The
ball went in.

"YES!" I yelled.

The whistle blew. The game was over.
The Bruisers had kicked butt—without
Chuckie. We were the champions!

Coach bought us sundaes, with the works. Lucy and I had everything on ours—sprinkles, strawberries, blueberries, chocolate sauce, marshmallow sauce, and caramel. Three scoops of ice cream, each. It was gross. It was perfect.

Derek said, "Hey, Coach, I can't finish my sundae."

"No problem," Chuckie said. "I'll do it." Chuckie finished Derek's sundae and Mikey's and one other kid's.

On the way home, Chuckie said, "Lucy and Willie, I've got to paint the front porch. Can you give me a hand?"

Lucy said, "Gee, Chuckie, we'd really like to help, but we're kind of tired."

"From scoring all those points," I said.

Lucy and I leaned against a tree in the empty lot across from Chuckie's house. We watched him get out the paint bucket,

the brushes, and a drop cloth. Then we
watched the thing that was better than any
TV show in the world. We watched
Chuckie paint his porch.

After that, we walked to Lucy's house to call Kyle and tell him how everything worked out. Lucy said, "Willie, I have a new song. Wanna hear?"

"Sure."

Willie and Lucy playing on a team
K-I-C-K-I-N-G
first comes passing
then comes scoring
then comes the Bruisers
with a big, fat trophy.

When it was safe, when no one could see, I put my arm around my bud.